The

Gingerbread House

by

Adèle Geras

Illustrated by Peter Bailey

You do not need to read this page -
just get on with the book!

Published in Great Britain by Barrington Stoke Ltd
10 Belford Terrace, Edinburgh, EH4 3DQ
First published in *Weird and Wonderful* by Orion Children's Books 1977

ISBN 1-84299-079-9

Printed by Polestar, Aberdeen

MEET THE AUTHOR - ADELE GERAS

What is your favourite animal?
Cat
What is your favourite boy's name?
Mark
What is your favourite girl's name?
Eleanor
What is your favourite food?
Indian
What is your favourite music?
Mozart
What is your favourite hobby?
Reading

MEET THE ILLUSTRATOR - PETER BAILEY

What is your favourite animal?
Cat
What is your favourite boy's name?
Tom
What is your favourite girl's name?
Anwen
What is your favourite food?
Curry
What is your favourite music?
Mozart
What is your favourite hobby?
Walking

For Wendy Cooling

Contents

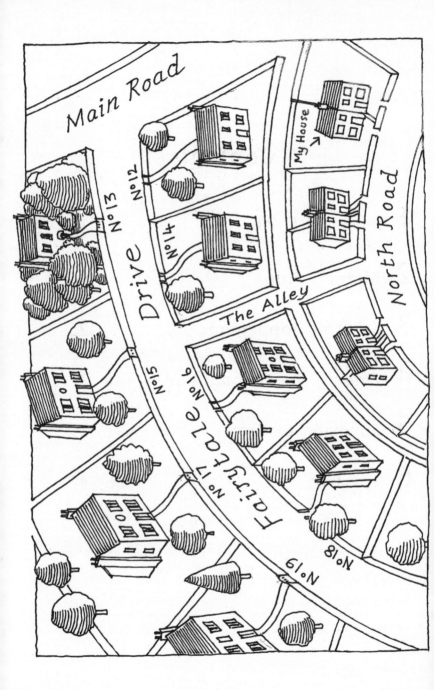

Chapter 1
Fairytale Drive

My name is Mike. I want to tell someone about Fairytale Drive, and what happened last year. If I don't, it will all be forgotten, like the hot weather we had ... remember that?

Fairytale Drive wasn't really called that, of course. Its proper name was Farradale Drive. Here is a map of it. I love stories that have maps to go with them. I've put in all the houses so that you know where everything is.

I live just through a little passageway we call 'The Alley' in North Road. Our houses are semis, and not big detached ones like the houses on Fairytale Drive. I can see the back of No. 12 from my bedroom window.

All the houses in Fairytale Drive have huge gardens. Luckily, most of them do not have very solid fences. We could creep through the gaps. This made things much easier for us last summer.

****

I suppose we were a gang, even though there were only three of us. I'm the only one left now that Midge and Toby have gone, and I miss them.

I am partly telling you about this as a way of remembering them, and partly I want to make a sort of confession. Even though I'm not sure that we did anything wrong.

Is it wrong to make things up? I don't mean lying or telling untruths to get something out of someone, or cheat them. I mean, inventing things, telling stories, recounting fantasies ... is that dangerous?

I think it is, a bit. I think if you tell things well enough, and make people believe them, they are halfway to coming true.

Midge was amazing. She never doubted any of her own stories. She would look you straight in the face. It was impossible not to be almost swallowed up in her pale, grey eyes. Then you would watch her mouth as it said the most impossible things. Half of you would want to laugh and say, "Come off it, Midge." The other half of you just had to believe her.

She looked very strange too. She was older than her brother Toby, who was in my class. She was nearly twelve, I think. Once I asked her how old she was and she just answered, "As old as the hills, Mike. Maybe older."

That was exactly the crazy sort of stuff Midge said all the time. Only you never told her it was crazy, and you never even thought it was, not while you were listening.

She was skinny and tall and freckled, with those eyes I've already mentioned. She had red hair. Midge's hair was the reddest I have ever seen. It hung down her back in two long plaits that looked dead old-fashioned.

I know a lot about girls. I have five girl cousins. You can call me sexist if you like, but they spend huge amounts of time and effort and talk on what they look like.

Midge was different. She never seemed to care, and she always looked the same in pale T-shirts and faded denim shorts.

Toby was short and plumpish and dark.
His hair was curly.

Midge used to say, "I don't look like
Toby because I'm a changeling. Do you
know what a changeling is? The fairies
come sometimes when a baby is really tiny.
They steal the human baby and put a fairy
baby in its place. I've always known that

Toby's parents are not my real parents. People with red hair are often changelings."

I said nothing. Well, what could I say? That Midge's mother looked just like her, only older? Midge would probably have kicked me.

People often pretend they're not really their parents' children. I had done it for a bit. When I was about seven, I had this Pretend Game that a Prince had given me to my mum and dad to take care of, but I always knew it *was* a Pretend Game and I stopped playing it after a while.

Chapter 2
Midge's Plan

The Fairytale Drive thing happened because there wasn't enough to do last summer. It was so hot. We couldn't be bothered to go to the park. Getting the bus into town was sticky and horrible and we couldn't face it. We did go swimming, and that was great. But we could only go when someone felt like taking us in the car, because the pool was so far away.

This left hours and hours for mooching around in.

Midge, because she was older, was the one in charge. She was always the one who decided what we did. She was the one who told us about Fairytale Drive.

We were sitting on the low wall outside No. 18, in the shade of a big tree, and Midge said, "You know No. 12. Who lives there?"

"It's Mrs Gardener," said Toby. "I know her. She's got a pointy nose and grey hair."

"She's got two grown-up daughters," I said. "I've seen them. One is fat and has sticky-out teeth."

"And the other is skinny and spotty," said Toby.

"Have you ever seen the third daughter?" Midge asked. "The youngest? She's very pretty."

"I've never seen a pretty one," I said. "Are you sure, Midge?"

"Sure as eggs is eggs," said Midge. "You never see her because she does all the housework. She's Cinderella."

"Whatever are you talking about?" I asked. "I think the heat's melted your brains."

Midge shook her head, and then she told us all about Fairytale Drive. She went from house to house. That fat man in No. 10, with the very pink face and the flattened nose

was actually the Third Little Pig. Hadn't we seen the hairy workman hanging around outside his house? Well, that was The Wolf, of course.

No. 14 had all those students. It was a little odd that there were seven, short, young men and only one woman in that house.

Hadn't we noticed her dark, dark, hair and very pale skin? Obviously, she was Snow White. "It stands to reason," was the way Midge put it.

On and on she went, talking and talking while the afternoon burned on. As she spoke, we got caught up in her tales and never noticed the heat.

That old bearded chap in No. 16, for instance, had just got married to a pretty woman who was much younger than he was. Had we ever heard of Bluebeard? He chopped up his brides, one after another ...

"I can easily imagine him having a lot of dead wives in a locked room," Midge said. "Can you?"

We could, at least while Midge was telling her stories.

We watched the old man go in and out of her house. His beard *did* have a definitely blue-ish tinge to it, Midge said.

I agreed with her. I hated the way he scowled at us. His eyes seemed almost yellow. And we often saw his wife, staring out of the window.

"She is waiting for her brothers to come and rescue her," Midge said. "She knows the secret her husband is hiding. She knows she is next. Will they come in time and save her?"

We really hoped they would. We watched out for them.

Then a van pulled up.

****

"See that?" said Midge. "Macintosh Fish. Fresh daily. That's what it says," she nodded.

A small man got out of the van and walked up to the front door.

"That's Mr Macintosh," Midge whispered. "Wait till you see his wife. She bosses him around. She's enormous and nags him all the time. I've heard her. Nothing's good enough for her. Before he found the Magic Fish they lived in a slum. He saved the Magic Fish's life by throwing it back into the sea. Now it grants his wishes. You'll see. The Macintoshes won't stay in Fairytale Drive long. Mrs Macintosh is too greedy. She's got to ask the Magic Fish for a palace soon, and then they'll be off."

That's how the game began, and we played it all summer. We pretended that every house in the Drive belonged not to ordinary people, but to characters from fairy stories.

Sometimes we saw a young girl with long hair at the highest window of No. 20. She was Rapunzel, naturally, and her mother would not let her go out with her boyfriend. Midge said she would most likely climb out of the window and run away with him. So it went on.

All summer long we crept in and out of people's gardens and spied on them.

****

I'm ashamed of it now. I don't think it's a nice thing to do, to go looking into people's windows, but Midge had made it all right. She had made it seem no worse than wandering through Disneyland.

"We're not touching anything," she used to say. "We're doing no harm."

We may not have been doing harm, but there is something dishonest about it, isn't there? I think there is something creepy about people not knowing that you are looking at them.

Chapter 3
Strange Happenings

I suppose we might have got fed up with the game quite quickly. But the strange thing was that the more we looked, the more real evidence we seemed to be collecting that our neighbours were indeed exactly the characters Midge had told us they were.

We saw Cinderella down on her hands and knees scrubbing the floor as if Hoovers and polishers hadn't been invented.

One day, we found the hairy workman
with his big, hairy hands pressed up
against Mr Pig's French windows.

"The Pig who built his house of bricks
lives here," Midge said. "And that workman
is Mr Wolf. The two other little pigs are
probably in his stomach already."

We never heard him say, "Little Pig,
Little Pig, let me come in", or "I'll huff and

I'll puff and I'll blow your house down".
But he looked as though he might say it at
any moment.

Once, we stared into Snow White's front
window. We could not see any of the short,
young men anywhere. An old woman with
horrid fingernails like red claws was sitting
at the dining-room table. She was showing
off a whole lot of jewellery. Snow White's
skin looked paler than ever.

"And look!" Midge whispered. "There's the Magic Comb. Can you see it? The teeth of the comb have been dipped in poison. Snow White will buy it and put it in her hair. She will die if no-one comes to save her."

We ran to the road. Maybe the young men were already on their way home.

So it went on. A 'For Sale' sign appeared outside the Macintosh house.

"I expect the Magic Fish has found them a palace," said Midge. "But Mrs Macintosh will soon get tired of that. She will want something even grander."

We believed her. Everything fitted. Everything worked. We had our own private TV serials going on around us all day long.

Chapter 4

Finding the Gingerbread House

But it wasn't Midge who found the Gingerbread House. I did that. It was on the corner of Fairytale Drive and the main road, and I don't know why Midge left it out of our games. It's true that you could hardly see it from anywhere in the Drive, and that was because there were trees and huge shrubs growing right up to the doors and windows.

My mum had a thing about the house. Every time we passed it, she would mutter something about Mrs Ellison living in the dark like a mole. "How can anyone live without light like that?" she'd say. "Those branches cover up all the downstairs windows."

"Do you know her?" I asked my mum.

"Not really," she said. "I know of her. She fosters children who need a home for a short time, when their parents find it hard to look after them for some reason."

Even though I knew about the fostering, I never mentioned it to Midge and Toby.

That afternoon, we saw the two small children arriving at the house surrounded by trees. They stood for a couple of seconds in the road, looking lost and white-faced, and I couldn't help saying what I said next.

They looked just like Hansel and Gretel, so I said, "They're Hansel and Gretel, aren't they, Midge, and that's the Gingerbread House."

She stared at them for a while, and then turned to me and smiled. Midge didn't smile very often, but when she did, you felt you had been given a special present.

"Yes, Mike," she said. "Yes." And then she murmured, "It was clever of you to spot the house in the forest. I've known it's a witch's house for some time. I've seen the kids. They come and they're skinny and miserable, and then they get plumper and much happier and then they disappear." She stared at me. "I didn't mention it because Toby gets nightmares, but you know, Mike, don't you ... what happens to those children?"

I nodded and shivered, even though the sun was shining. Half of me, most of me, was thinking, what a load of rubbish!

Of course the children get plump. Mrs Ellison is kind and feeds them well and looks after them properly.

Of course they disappear. They're only being fostered for a while, until they can go back home to their real parents again.

Of course they don't stay long.

Of course new children keep coming.

There was a perfectly normal explanation for everything.

I should have said so to Midge, but I kept quiet. I revelled in the idea of a witch living so close to us.

I believed in Hansel and Gretel more than in any of the other inhabitants of Fairytale Drive.

I lay in bed and thought about Gretel pushing the witch into the oven. I couldn't get the idea of Hansel in his cage out of my dreams.

Chapter 5
Speaking to Gretel

We were sitting on the wall one day, bored with all the other houses, and moaning about not being able to get into Mrs Ellison's garden, which Midge called 'The Forest'. The gate was locked (we didn't know why), the fence was high and there were no gaps to slip through.

"There's Gretel," Midge said suddenly. "Let's talk to her."

"No," I cried, thinking, *that's against the rules*. I think I was frightened that our fairytales might vanish into thin air if we ever actually talked to anyone.

I was too late. Midge had gone up to the gate and was talking to the little girl. "Hello," Midge said. "What's your name?"

"Greta," said the girl. A cloud appeared in the sky and covered up the sun, and in the shade of the trees we were almost in darkness.

"How old are you?" Midge asked.

"Five."

"Where's your brother?"

"Inside," said the little girl. Greta.

"Why doesn't he come out and play?" Midge asked.

"He can't," said Greta.

"Why not?"

"Mrs Ellison said so. He's tired."

"Do you like it here?" Midge said.

"Yes," said Greta. Then, "I want Mummy."

"Is Mrs Ellison kind to you?" I asked.

Greta nodded. "She makes cakes. I like cakes. She lets me help her."

The side door of the Gingerbread House opened, and there was Mrs Ellison herself. She wore a black dress. She smiled at me. Her teeth were like small tombstones, and her eyes made you shiver. I felt that they could see right through me.

"Come inside now, Greta," she smiled, and she waved at us. "Hello, children! It's time for Greta's supper."

Her voice reminded me of chalk scraped on a blackboard. The little girl turned and walked to where Mrs Ellison was standing.

"Look!" Midge whispered. "She's frightened. She doesn't want to go ..."

I looked at Midge. Her grey eyes were burning, and her face was quite white. She turned to me and Toby. "We must tell someone," she said. "I'm really scared. We must tell your mum, Mike."

****

So we did. We went to my house and told her. Not everything of course. We said nothing about Fairytale Drive, or Hansel or Gretel. My mum would have thought we were mad. All we said was we thought the little girl looked frightened, and was she sure Mrs Ellison was not mistreating her in some way.

My mum's got as many faults as anyone else's mother, but she does listen. She takes what you say seriously.

She listened. She told us not to judge Mrs Ellison by how she looked. She said it was easy to imagine things. She told us that Mrs Ellison had been fostering children for years. She told us not to worry.

I felt much happier. Midge and Toby went home, so I don't know how they felt.

Later, when my dad came home, my mum said, "I worry about Midge sometimes. I think perhaps she needs some help. It can't be healthy to spend so much time imagining things. I'll speak to her mother about it."

I went to bed feeling happy. I knew that tonight I would not dream of a skinny boy locked up in a metal cage.

Chapter 6
The Fire

The fire engines woke me up. I ran to the window and the whole sky was red. Even in the house, the smell of burning nearly choked us. My parents were up, and in their dressing-gowns. Someone was shouting.

I had never seen a real fire before, and I wanted to go out and have a look, but my mother wouldn't let me.

"Whose house is it?" I asked. "Do you know whose house it is?"

My mum looked as if she'd been crying. "It's Mrs Ellison's," she said.

I said nothing.

I just looked out of the window at the night that was suddenly no longer dark.

I couldn't get rid of the pictures in my mind, pictures of Mrs Ellison being pushed into her own oven. Stop! I told myself. Her cooker is probably modern and electric. Stop this nonsense ... it's a game. It's only a game.

In the end, there was nothing else to see, and I went to bed. The last thought I had before I fell asleep was to wonder whether Midge and Toby had seen the fire. They must have done. The whole street must have seen it.

The day after the fire, my mum told me that poor Mrs Ellison had died.

"Are the children all right?" I asked.

"Yes," said my mum. "Thank God. They've gone back to their parents. It must have been terrible for them."

I sat on the wall that afternoon with Midge and Toby and told them what my mum had said. Toby was silent. Midge looked at the burned-out blackened shell of the Gingerbread House and said only, "It stands to reason."

We never played the Fairytale Drive game again. Midge and Toby left a couple of weeks later. Their dad had found a job in Japan and their house was up for sale.

In the middle of October, someone bought the ruins of the Gingerbread House

and its garden. The trees were cut down. Bulldozers came in and started clearing away what was left of the building.

I stood in the road and looked at it after it was all flattened out. The new owner saw me. He invited me to have a look. Then he went off somewhere.

I was left alone. There was a chunk of old chimney lying around in the earth. I moved it with my foot.

Then I saw them. I picked them up and put them in my trouser pockets.

I knew it was wrong to go back there the next day. There was no-one around.

I have never told anyone about what I found. I had to collect the others. I made sure to take a carrier bag.

There were sixteen altogether, scorched, charred to blackness, and scattered all over the place by the builders. Children's shoes. Very small children's shoes.

Maybe Mrs Ellison's foster children had left them behind when they went home. Or maybe not.

I know which story Midge would have believed.

****

One day when Mum was out, I dug a hole in the garden and buried the shoes in it, and said a prayer over them.

Just in case.

Barrington Stoke was a famous and much-loved story-teller. He travelled from village to village carrying a lantern to light his way. He arrived as it grew dark and when the young boys and girls of the village saw the glow of his lantern, they hurried to the central meeting place. They were full of excitement and expectation, for his stories were always wonderful.

Then Barrington Stoke set down his lantern. In the flickering light the listeners were enthralled by his tales of adventure, horror and mystery. He knew exactly what they liked best and he loved telling a good story. And another. And then another. When the lantern burned low and dawn was nearly breaking, he slipped away. He was gone by morning, only to appear the next day in some other village to tell the next story.

If you loved this story, why don't you read . . .

Ship of Ghosts

by Nigel Hinton

Have you sometimes longed for excitement and adventure? Mick has wanted to go to sea ever since he learned that his Dad was a sailor. His dreams come true. But what he discovers on the Ship of Ghosts turn his dreams into a nightmare.

"This is compelling reading" *The Guardian*

You can order this book directly from:
Macmillan Distribution Ltd, Brunel Road, Houndmills,
Basingstoke, Hampshire RG21 6XS
Tel: 01256 302699